DOGNAPPED!

BOOKS IN THE PUPPY PATROL™ SERIES

DOGNAPPED!

JENNY DALE

Illustrations by Mick Reid
Cover illustration by Michael Rowe

AN
APPLE
PAPERBACK

SCHOLASTIC INC.
New York Toronto London Auckland Sydney
Mexico City New Delhi Hong Kong Buenos Aires

No part of this publication may be reproduced, in whole or in part, or stored in a retrieval system, or transmitted in any form or by any means, electronic, mechanical, photocopying, recording, or otherwise, without written permission of the publisher. For information regarding permission, write to Macmillan Publishers Ltd., 20 New Wharf Rd., London N1 9RR Basingstoke and Oxford.

ISBN 0-439-45350-X

Text copyright © 2000 by Working Partners Limited.
Illustrations copyright © 2000 by Mick Reid.

All rights reserved. Published by Scholastic Inc., 557 Broadway, New York, NY 10012 by arrangement with Macmillan Children's Books, a division of Macmillan Publishers Ltd.

SCHOLASTIC and associated logos are trademarks and/or registered trademarks of Scholastic Inc.

12 11 10 9 8 7 6 5 4 3 2 1   3 4 5 6 7 8/0

Printed in the U.S.A.   40
First Scholastic printing, July 2003

SPECIAL THANKS TO MARGARET MCALLISTER

DOGNAPPED!

CHAPTER ONE

The green King Street Kennels Range Rover bumped up the uneven road to Priorsfield Farm and came to a stop in the farmyard. Neil Parker jumped down and held out his arms to the black-and-tan dog that was racing eagerly toward him.

"Hi, Bramble! Remember me?"

As he bent down to say hello, the spirited little dog leaped up and licked his cheek in an enthusiastic doggy greeting.

Neil's mother, Carole, heaved two bulky packs of dog food out of the back of the car. "Keep an eye on Jake, Emily," she called to Neil's younger sister. "I don't think Harry will want him running loose on his farm — he's a four-legged danger zone!"

Jake, Neil's black-and-white Border collie, was already barking in indignation at having to stay in the car while Neil fussed over another dog. Neil Parker was just about the biggest dog fan in the small town of Compton. His family ran King Street Kennels, a boarding kennel and dog rescue center, and sometimes it seemed like Neil thought about nothing but dogs.

He whistled for Jake and quickly snapped his leash on, then passed it to ten-year-old Emily while he went to help his mom with the dog food.

"Can I help, too?" asked the baby of the Parker family, five-year-old Sarah, clambering out of the car.

"You can help me with Jake if you want, Squirt. We'll go and visit the ducks," said Emily. "I think Neil can manage."

Neil grimaced as he picked up one of the heavy bags and headed toward the farmhouse with Bramble at his heel.

The farmer, Harry Grey, came striding out of a nearby barn mopping his brow with a large handkerchief. He was a tall man, lean and weatherbeaten, with his bright-eyed Jack Russell terrier, Tuff, following at his heels.

As soon as he spotted Bramble, Tuff raced toward him. The two dogs chased each other excitedly in circles and disappeared off toward the barn.

"He's a great little dog, that Bramble." Harry Grey

smiled as he watched them go. "He and Tuff are best friends. You did me a big favor there, Neil."

Neil had a particular interest in Bramble. The dog had once belonged to two local brothers — poachers who had abandoned Bramble tangled deep inside a blackberry bush. Neil had rescued the dog, and the two poachers were later prosecuted and banned from keeping animals. Bramble had been adopted by the Grey family as a working dog and had soon recovered from the neglect he had suffered.

"Those dogs are certainly full of energy," said Carole. "I've brought your dog food over, Harry. It was delivered to us by mistake."

"That's very kind of you, Carole!" said Harry. "Put those heavy bags down — I'll take them indoors later."

Neil put his bag down, picked up a stick, and whistled. Bramble and Tuff wheeled around and raced toward him as he sent the stick flying through the air. They pounced on it and fought a tug-of-war. Bramble won and brought it back to Neil to throw again.

"I've just discovered something new about our Bramble," said Harry Grey with satisfaction. "Neil, what breed of dog do you think he is?"

"Breed?" It hadn't occurred to Neil that Bramble had a breed at all. He just seemed like a tough little mutt. Taking a closer look at him now, Neil noticed

his well-shaped muzzle, his smooth dark coat, his lean, long body, and, for the first time, the strong frame of his jaw. With a violent shake of his head, Bramble broke the stick in two.

"I suppose he's got a lot of terrier in him," Neil guessed. "Fox terrier, maybe. And perhaps a bit of beagle. And maybe a bit of Jack Russell, same as Tuff."

"That's what I always thought," said the farmer, "but Mike Turner, the vet, was here the other day to look at the new lambs, and he thinks our mutt isn't a mutt at all. He's a German hunting terrier."

"A what?" said Neil.

"Really?" said Carole.

"You don't see many of them around," said Harry Grey. "Apparently, Mike's brother used to own one. They're working dogs, not pets. Meant for hunting rats and the like."

"And he belonged to those two poachers!" exclaimed Neil.

"Carl and Gary Smith," said the farmer. "Makes you wonder where they got hold of a dog like that, doesn't it?" He looked past them as Tuff ran to meet Emily and Sarah, who were on their way back from the pond. Sarah was tugging at Emily's hand, pulling her on.

"Mom, there are lots of baby ones! Little fluffy ducklings, all bobbing up and down on the water! Come and see!"

"Mostly mallards," said Emily knowledgeably. "And a family of moorhens. They're just little bobbles of fluff." Jake barked. "I think Jake likes them, too," she added, smiling.

"I suppose you'd like to see the new lambs, too?" said Harry Grey, and chuckled at the delight on Sarah's face. "Come on, then. We'll go to the lambing shed."

The lambing shed was a long, low building on the opposite side of the yard. The lambing season was well underway, and the adjoining field was filled with ewes and new lambs bleating in high, demand-

ing voices. A small flock stood in one corner. The lambs, with their soft, white fleeces and gentle, inquisitive faces, stayed close to their mothers, their feet splayed and their little tails wagging.

"Sweet!" exclaimed Emily.

"Just wait till you see the lambing shed," said Harry Grey. "Now make sure to shut all the gates. We can't have Tuff or Bramble running around here. Come on in, but be very quiet."

The shed seemed dimly lit and warm compared to the bright, breezy spring morning. A heavy, sweet smell of straw and animals hung in the air. On both sides were rows of roomy pens, some empty, others with patient ewes lying in the straw.

In the pen nearest to them, a large and shaggy ewe lay on her side with a creamy-yellow lamb curled fast asleep beside her. Its small black nose was tucked in tightly against its tummy.

Carole nudged Neil and pointed to the opposite pen. A tall, elderly man with a bush of straggly white hair and a beard was bent over an ewe. Harry Grey went to join them, and squatted down in the straw as he gently talked to the ewe.

"Good girl," the farmer reassured her. "She's nearly there, Nick."

"The lamb's back to front," muttered the old man, glancing up. His sharp features were twisted with worry.

Neil recognized him. It was Nick, the eccentric old man who had once found a lost dog they were looking for and who had ended up spending Christmas at King Street. Nobody seemed to know his last name, but Sarah thought he looked like Santa Claus, and the name "Nick Christmas" stuck.

"Breech presentation," whispered Carole to Neil. "That means the lamb's the wrong way around. It'll be born with its bottom first or its hind feet first. It could be difficult."

The ewe strained her head back. Neil held Jake tightly by his side. He and Emily watched a wet, pinky-yellow bulge being pushed out into Nick's expectant hands. Gently and skillfully, he eased it out and they saw the tiny hooves, the thin legs, and finally the rumpled head of the newborn lamb.

"Well done, girl," said Nick. He smiled as he took a handful of straw and rubbed the slithery lamb clean and dry. He seemed delighted that everything had gone smoothly.

Neil glimpsed the newborn lamb's tight curls and creamy coat as Nick laid it beside its mother. She sniffed at her offspring curiously, and began to lick it.

Sarah's eyes bulged with fascination. "Will it be OK?"

Harry Grey laughed softly. "It's a very healthy little girl, Sarah, an ewe lamb. We'll name it after you, how about that?"

Sarah's face grew even brighter as she looked radiantly up at him.

Nick grinned, and nodded before going to check on the other sheep in the shed.

"Nick's helping me with the lambing," said the farmer. "He's very good with sheep. Picked up all the old shepherding skills when he was younger. He says he'll stay here as long as the season lasts, then take off again. I don't think he likes to be in one place for too long." He called over his shoulder, "You go and clean up and take a break, Nick. You've been up all night. I'll see to things here."

Sarah was gazing lovingly at the lamb. "I wish Jake was a sheepdog," she said. "Then we could come here all the time."

Farmer Grey looked at Jake, then laughed. "I wouldn't let young Jake off the leash anywhere near these lambs. He'd cause havoc," he said, and led the way out of the lambing shed. They all leaned on the gate to watch the lambs in the field. "Border collies make good sheepdogs because they have the instinct to chase things," continued Harry. "That's why untrained ones can be troublemakers. "Tuff and Bramble should not get near the sheep, either."

"Tuff and Bramble have enough to do keeping rats away," said Neil.

"That's right. They chase anything! That's why," he added thoughtfully, "at this time of year I need to keep the gate shut between them and the ducks. Tuff doesn't know what's vermin and what's not. If it's small and runs away, chase it — that's his understanding."

"Oh, no!" said Emily, who couldn't bear to think of any animal being hurt.

Neil looked across the adjacent field and noticed a large black-and-white collie ambling peacefully from the gate toward Nick's trailer. Her coat was shaggy with age, and turning to brown and yellow in places.

"You're being honored, Neil. Cap's come to say hello," Harry said. Cap was Harry's retired sheepdog. She was too old and deaf to herd sheep any more, but Neil had trained her to respond to hand signals.

"Can I go in the field?" he asked, and as soon as Harry nodded Neil was running across to Cap.

Before he could reach her, Neil noticed something had suddenly caught the collie's attention. Cap was alert, staring at the edge of the field, her head down. Neil couldn't see what she'd spotted, but as he came closer he could make out a bundle wrapped in a discarded shred of dirty old curtain by the hedge. The curtain was off-white with a pattern of purple flowers, and, he noticed with a shiver, it was blood-stained.

Cap crept up on it and was there before him. She thrust her muzzle into the bundle, backed away, and gave a low, warning bark. With rising anxiety Neil lurched forward. He kneeled beside the bundle and cautiously looked to see what Cap had found.

Neil saw smooth white hair, thickly matted with darkening blood. With relief, he noticed, too, a barely moving flank. Whatever lay in there was still breathing. He felt someone's presence and turned to see Nick Christmas bending over his shoulder with shock and concern on his face. Emily was running toward them.

"Someone call the vet!" shouted Neil. "It's an emergency!"

CHAPTER TWO

Neil felt his stomach tighten as he carefully lifted back the ragged strip of curtain.

It was a dog.

Its eyes were barely open, and its breathing was shallow and labored. Blood had dried on the deep gashes across its neck and shoulder, and its right foreleg was a torn and bleeding mess.

Neil had seen injured dogs in the past, and ill-treated and neglected dogs, too. But he had never seen anything as bad as this.

"What happened to you?" Neil whispered, hardly daring to move or stroke the dog for fear of hurting it. "All right, you're going to be OK now. We've found you." He put one arm around Cap and gave her a hug of congratulations. "Good job, girl."

Nick squatted down beside them, muttering something under his breath as he helped Neil to lift the wounded dog. They kept the curtain wrapped around it in order to disturb it as little as possible. Emily, who had just caught up with them, looked at the dog and her expression changed from concern to horror.

"Oh, you poor dog! What a shame! It's all right now, we've got you." Jake barked and Emily held him back. She turned and ran back across the field toward the yard. As Neil followed slowly behind, he saw her take Sarah by the hand. Though his attention was on the dog in his arms, he was aware of Emily leading Sarah toward the lambing shed. Emily had made the right decision. Sarah was too young to see a dog with such appalling injuries.

Harry Grey and Carole didn't wait to see the injured dog. Carole was already opening the doors of the Range Rover, and the farmer took the dog gently in his arms while Neil got into the car.

Carole glanced at the gashes in the bloodied white coat. "Keep him warm, Neil," she said, as Harry Grey handed the dog over. "He's in shock. There'll be a blanket or a towel or something in the back. Where's Sarah?"

"She can stay here," said Harry. "She'll be no bother. It's best to keep her out of this, and she's no trouble. Emily and Jake, too."

Nick Christmas stood at the farmer's shoulder, his face etched with anxiety. "Shouldn't do that," he grumbled, more to himself than to anyone else. "It's all wrong."

The dog in Neil's arms gave a thin whine of distress. Its eyes flickered open and shut.

"Hang in there," said Harry as he shut the door.

Carole drove slowly through the gate and along the farm road. "I'll take this stretch at an easy pace," she said. "It'll slow us down, but I don't want to jolt the dog around and hurt him." Her eyes glanced toward the clock on the dashboard. "Find my cell and phone the office number at King Street, Neil. Mike should still be doing his Saturday morning clinic."

Kate Paget, the kennel assistant, was in the King Street office. Neil, not taking his eyes off the dog, told her what had happened and asked her to take a message to Mike Turner, the vet.

"While you're talking to Kate," cut in Carole, "tell her it's a Staffordshire bull terrier."

Neil hadn't even thought about the dog's breed, but, now that his mom mentioned it, he knew she was right. He noticed the distinctive patchy markings and its square head. The dog was solidly boned and muscular, heavy in his arms for its size.

"What d'you think happened to him?" asked Neil after he had hung up the phone. He bent over the dog. "Road accident? Caught on barbed wire?"

"Those gashes look too deep for barbed wire," said Carole.

"Do you think he's been attacked by something?" said Neil.

"Whatever it is," his mom replied as they turned onto the main road and gathered speed, "he didn't wrap himself up in a curtain and leave himself where Nick or Harry was sure to find him. Something's going on."

As the Range Rover parked at King Street Kennels, Kate Paget ran out to meet them. "Mike says to take him straight into the clinic," she said. She ushered Neil past the pets and owners in the waiting room. "There's no time to lose. Let's get him on the operating table."

Carole said she'd go back to the farm to pick up Emily, Sarah, and Jake.

"Sorry, everyone, I'm afraid you may have to wait a little longer," Kate boomed to the waiting customers. "We have an emergency here."

Within a minute, Neil was lowering the dog onto Mike's operating table.

"What a horror!" Mike said as he unwrapped the tattered curtain with great care and examined the animal's gashes. "I'll treat him for the pain and shock first, then, when he's stable, we'll see about getting him stitched up. He's dehydrated, too. We'll need to set up a drip, Kate, to get some fluids into him. And he's lost a lot of blood. From the quantity of dried blood, I'd say these injuries happened several hours ago. Tell me exactly where he was, Neil, and how you found him."

Neil described the time and place precisely. Before he had finished, his father had arrived. Bob, tall, broad-shouldered, and bearded, had a more thorough understanding of dogs than anyone Neil had ever met. He looked at the dog, then gravely at Mike.

"I'll do what I can, Bob," said Mike. "The dog will have to do the rest himself, and I'm not sure that he's up to it."

"It may just be a case of making him comfortable for as long as he lasts, Neil," said Bob very quietly. "He looks bad."

His father's low voice alerted Neil. He could see that his dad wasn't just concerned about this dog — he was quietly angry as well.

"I hadn't noticed anything until Cap saw him," said Neil. "And Nick had been in the lambing shed all morning, so he wouldn't have seen anything. What do you think happened to him, Mike?"

Mike and Bob exchanged glances and nodded briefly.

"These wounds may have been caused by another dog," said Mike. "They're very deep and severe. I think we should get the SPCA involved immediately."

"I'll phone Terri McCall," Kate said, and left.

"Why do you need the SPCA officer?" asked Neil. "If two dogs fight, it can't be a cruelty case, can it?"

"This one could be," said Bob. For a long time he said nothing else — only studied the dog's injuries as if he wanted to be sure of something. "I hoped we'd never, ever see anything like this. Come on, Neil, you've delivered him into safe hands. We'll let Mike get on with his job now."

They were nearly out of the clinic when Kate returned. "I got Terri on her cell," she said. "She was on her way anyway. She has some news."

"Neil, we need to talk about this," said Bob.

Neil gave the dog a last look. He was sleeping peacefully. "Hold on, boy," he said. "Put up a fight."

"That's the last thing he needs to do," muttered Bob mysteriously, and together they walked back to the office where Carole and Emily had just arrived.

"Neil, Emily," said Bob, taking a seat behind the desk and looking at them seriously, "are you aware of such a thing as organized dogfights?"

"They used to do that with pit bull terriers, didn't they?" said Emily. "But it's banned now."

"It's not that simple," said Carole. "Dogfighting still goes on. It's illegal, but it still happens. It just happens in secret now."

"So you think the dog got those wounds in a fight? That someone *deliberately* let this happen?" said Neil. He hoped it wasn't true. He ignored the sick, churning feeling that was growing in his stomach. "There must be some other explanation, right?"

"Look at the severity of the wounds," said Bob gently. "And he's a bull terrier. If the sick people who organize dogfights can't get pit bulls, they go for the next best thing."

"And somebody left him to be found," Carole pointed out. "Somebody who realized he needed help, and perhaps had a guilty conscience but didn't want to bring the dog to a vet who'd ask awkward questions." There was the sound of a van parking outside. "That must be Terri — she got here quickly."

Neil, followed by Jake, went outside to find Terri.

Jake would usually bound up to her, sure of an enthusiastic welcome, but even he seemed strangely subdued — aware that everyone was in a very gloomy and serious mood.

"Hello, Jake. Hi, Neil. Kate called me on the cell to say that you've got a casualty on your hands. A potential cruelty case."

"Yes, Mike and Kate are with him now," said Neil. "They're not hopeful about his chances."

Terri sat down in the office while Carole made coffee. "I was on my way over here anyway. I came to warn Mike to be extra careful about security at the clinic. Jill Walker — the vet in Padsham — had her clinic broken into last night."

Emily, who was sitting on the floor fussing over Jake, looked up. "Who'd break into a vet's clinic?" she asked. "Were they after money?"

"No. Medication," said Terri.

"But who would want to steal medicine that's only useful for treating animals?" asked Emily.

Neil tried to think it through, but his mind was on the wounded dog in the operating room. Carole was just beginning to tell Terri what had happened when Kate arrived.

"Mike's got the dog sedated and stitched," she said quietly. Her face was grave.

Neil, Emily, and Terri went with her to the clinic.

"What are the dog's chances?" asked Terri.

"Not good," admitted Kate. "The wounds are deep

and he's lost a lot of blood. And he was left untreated overnight."

"He has to make it!" cried Emily. "At least he has to know that somebody cared enough to rescue him!"

The small room Mike used as the King Street clinic was plain and neat, with a smell of freshly scrubbed disinfectant. The dog lay in a pen, cushioned on a blanket. Sedated, he looked very peaceful in spite of the severe wounds stitched across his back and leg.

Terri bent over him to take a careful look, then she looked past the dog to Mike. She repeated her news to him about the break-in. "They took anti-inflammatories, antibiotics, and syringes," she added. "And now we find a dog in this condition. It certainly seems to me to fit a pattern. They probably thought this dog was beyond repair. What do you think, Mike?"

"I definitely think we should involve the police," said Mike in a voice quiet with controlled anger. "I'll call Sergeant Moorhead."

Neil remembered how well the day had started with his visit to Priorsfield Farm — watching the lambs and meeting some of his old doggy friends again. It was only an hour ago, but it seemed like a week. Now, he was facing the appalling possibility of there being dogfighting going on right on his own doorstep.

CHAPTER THREE

"**I**'m afraid there might be an organized ring," said Terri.

"A ring?" Until now, Neil had imagined two men in a back room somewhere, setting dogs against each other as some kind of sick bet. "What do you mean, a ring?"

Terri stood in the King Street Kennels clinic and shook her head, as if the thought was too unpleasant for her. "Dogfighting," she said, "is a highly organized business. At the top level, they breed and sell dogs especially for fighting. Otherwise, they choose dogs that look suitable — like this one, a Staffy — and train them."

"But that's . . ." Neil was enraged and struggled

for words. "It's horrible! They can't do that! It must be against the law, isn't it?"

"Of course it is," Terri replied, "but that doesn't stop certain people from trying it. They are very secretive, and they make money from trading dogs and betting on fights." She turned to the vet. "Mike, I don't want to disturb the Staffy, but I'll need to take photographs. I'll use them to support a case, if we manage to bring anyone to court over this."

Neil stroked the dog's head as Terri stepped back with a camera she pulled out from her bag. She crouched down, moving from one angle to another to get the clearest view of the gashed shoulder and the torn leg. Neil made soft shushing noises to keep the dog calm.

"We've got to find the people responsible for this!" he urged Terri.

"I know that, but it's not easy," she said. "All we've got is one dog with injuries from bites. It isn't much to go on, except that he's a fighting breed, and was found in suspicious circumstances."

"Isn't that enough?" said Neil, keeping his voice low for the sake of the dog.

Terri moved to the other side of the pen to get a different view. "Not in court, it isn't," she said. "But then, there's the question of the break-in at Jill's."

"I don't get it," said Emily. "What's that got to do with it?"

"If you've used a dog for fighting and it gets injured," said Terri, "you're not going to take it to a vet, who might realize exactly how those injuries happened. People involved in rings usually treat their dogs themselves, sometimes using nasty homemade concoctions that can do more harm than good. But, if they can, they get hold of the right sort of medication."

"Oh, I see," said Emily. "By stealing from a vet."

"Exactly," said Terri, and clicked the shutter once more. "OK, that's all the pictures I need, Neil. Close the pen and we'll leave this poor wounded soldier in peace."

Together they walked outside. "Isn't there anything else we can do now?" urged Neil. "Before another dog gets hurt?"

"I can't do everything instantly, Neil," said Terri. "I need to find out for sure if there is a dogfighting ring, then I need enough evidence for the police to arrest the culprits and prosecute them."

"Then we'll have to move fast," said Neil.

Terri stopped in the middle of unlocking her van. She turned to him sternly. "Now, Neil, get this firmly between your ears," she said. "I know you've helped me with cases in the past, and I appreciate that. But this is different. We're probably talking about some very dangerous criminals here. They may be violent, and I don't want you — or you, Emily — in the front line. This case is for me and the police. Got it?"

"And you could seriously snarl up Terri's investigation if you tried to help," added Carole. "So stay out of it."

That evening, just after the Parkers had finished dinner, Harry Grey arrived at King Street, anxious to hear the latest news about the savaged dog.

Carole Parker welcomed him in and he sat down at the kitchen table with a cup of coffee. Before anyone had had a chance to fill him in, Sarah came skipping into the room with something tangled in her hands and announced, "I've learned to knit!"

Neil's jaw dropped. "What?"

Emily giggled. "It's true, Neil."

Harry Grey smiled, too. "She was looking at my wife's knitting and was dying to try it. I think she started Sarah off!"

"Look!" Proudly, Sarah held up a tangled mess of yellow wool on two thick needles. To Neil, it looked like something Sarah's pet hamster, Fudge, had made a nest in, but Sarah seemed very pleased with it.

"What's it supposed to be?" Neil asked. Carole gave him a nudge with her elbow.

"It's very good, Sarah," her mother said.

"I've only just started," said Sarah. "It's going to be a blanket."

"I'm sure it'll be a beautiful one," said Carole, and smiled across at Mr. Grey.

Harry cleared his throat. "So, how is he?"

"It's pretty grim," said Carole with a frown. "Mike's patched him up, but it's touch and go. It's possible that he was out in that field all night."

"Did you hear anything last night?" inquired Neil. "A car engine, maybe?"

"When you've been up night after night with the lambs, you could sleep through a hurricane," said the farmer. "Sorry, Neil, I can't help you. I didn't hear a thing, and the dogs were in kennels at the back of the house, so they must not have noticed anything, either. Cap was in the trailer with Nick, but she's deaf. All I can tell you is that I went out at about eleven o'clock to check the sheep, and I didn't see anything then."

"If you do see anything suspicious again, will you let us know?" said Neil. "Terri says there may be a dogfighting ring somewhere around here."

"The Staffy's gone to Mike's clinic," said Emily. "We just hope he'll be OK."

"Mom," interrupted Sarah, "I don't think I've got enough wool for a blanket. Have you got any?"

"I have, yes." Carole smiled patiently. "I've got some odds and ends somewhere, but not enough for a blanket."

"I don't mean a whole big blanket," said Sarah. "I mean a dog-sized blanket. For one of the rescue dogs."

"That's very kind of you," said Carole.

"Or maybe for Jake," Sarah went on, gazing thoughtfully down at the snoozing collie in his basket.

"Or maybe for the Staffy," added Emily.

Neil smiled at her. "He doesn't have a name yet, does he? Or, at least, we don't know it."

Neil didn't want to tell Sarah how sick the dog was. But to him, the terrier didn't look as if he'd last long enough to need his own blanket.

The next morning was Sunday, which meant obedience class at King Street. Neil took Jake as usual, but it was hard to concentrate knowing that the

Staffordshire bull terrier in Mike's care was fighting for his life. Usually, after the class was finished, he stopped to talk to his friends among the dogs and their owners, but this time he called Jake and went straight back to the house.

"Any news?" Neil asked as soon as he was through the front door.

"Mike phoned," said Carole, and he could see she was troubled. "I'm sorry, Neil, but the Staffy's gotten worse."

"Worse!" He hung up Jake's leash. "How much worse can he be?"

"He's got an infection. Only to be expected, I'm afraid. Lying wrapped in a dirty rag with untreated bites. And on a cold night. Mike's got him pumped full of antibiotics, but he was already weak without this setback."

Neil glanced around the room. Sarah sat curled in a chair, knitting industriously at something like a lopsided cobweb.

"Mom, where's Emily?" asked Neil.

"She went to her room after Mike phoned," said Carole. "She doesn't want to talk to anyone."

However, just at that moment, Emily came into the kitchen. Her eyes looked pink. She kneeled down and held out her arms to hug Jake. "I heard you come in," she said to Neil. She wrapped her arms around Jake's comforting warmth. "Has Mom told you?"

"Yes," said Neil.

"We're calling him Titan," Emily said quietly.

"He couldn't just die and never have a name." She buried her face in Jake's coat.

The doorbell rang. Jake struggled away from Emily's arms and ran barking to the door as Neil opened it. Emily wiped her face quickly.

"Sergeant Moorhead!" said Neil. The police officer stood on the doorstep, tall and imposing in his uniform. "Come in — did you want to ask about the dog we found?"

"Yes. I hope I'm not interrupting Sunday lunch?" said the sergeant.

"Not at all," said Carole. She took a quick look inside the oven and turned it down. A delicious roasting smell reminded Neil that breakfast was a long time ago.

"I need all the information you can give me about the finding of this dog Mike's told me about," said the policeman. "I understand you got there first, Neil?"

Carole made coffee while Sergeant Moorhead listened to the story of how Titan was discovered. He scribbled notes now and then.

"The curious thing," he said, when he had heard everyone's part of the story, "is why somebody left him where he could be found. Dogfighting men usually treat injuries themselves, or just let the dogs die." There were gasps of outrage from Neil and Emily. "But anybody who really did care for the animal would have taken it to a vet. I don't suppose anyone kept the cloth he was wrapped in?"

"It's at the rescue center," said Neil. "It's a piece of dirty white curtain with purple flowers on it."

"I'll go get it, then, and leave you people in peace. If you hear anything else, let me know," said the sergeant.

"I hope we don't hear anything else," said Emily after he had gone. "I hope there isn't anything else to hear. I really, really want Terri to be wrong about all this, and for there to be no dogfighting. I don't want there to be anything so cruel and so near to us when we're not allowed to help."

"There won't be," said Neil, "not if we can stop it." He was so angry that Terri's warnings had already been forgotten.

By the time they went to bed that night, there was no improvement in Titan's condition. After a long and anxious day at school on Monday, Neil came home to hear the latest news.

"Mike called," said Carole. "Titan's still very weak, but he's responding to the antibiotics."

"Told you!" said Emily. "Told you he's a Titan!"

"It's still touch and go," Carole warned them. But Neil felt sure that Titan really had turned the corner.

He biked home quickly the following day, hoping for more equally good news. When he reached home,

Harry Grey's Land Rover was parked in the driveway, with Cap barking sharply in the back. Harry Grey was walking to the office as Bob came out to meet him.

"Bob," Harry was saying hurriedly as Neil caught up with him, "he hasn't turned up here, has he?"

"Sorry, who?" asked Bob.

There was puzzled anxiety on Harry's face. "I thought he might have been brought in," he said. "Bramble, I mean."

"Bramble?" said Neil.

"There's no sign of him anywhere! I think he must have run off, so I hoped somebody might have handed him in here." The farmer caught his breath. "He's disappeared!"

CHAPTER FOUR

The silence was scary. Neil immediately sensed what his father was thinking. He was thinking it himself.

Bob was the first to speak. "When did you first notice he was missing?" he asked Harry Grey.

"Hard to say, exactly. I noticed this morning that Tuff was all alone, but I knew my wife Angie had gone to mend a fence on the far side of the woods, so I assumed she'd taken Bramble with her. When she got back, I found out that she hadn't seen him all day, either."

"He's definitely disappeared?" asked Neil.

"I've searched everywhere," said Harry. "I've even taken Tuff with me to look for him. We went around all the warrens, even though Bramble's too big to get lost down a rabbit hole."

"I think you'd better sit down, Harry." Bob sighed. "Unfortunately, I think we might know what has happened to him."

In the office, Bob repeated to Harry all that Terri had said about the dogfighting. Harry said he had suspected as much, but was still clearly very distressed.

"We may be wrong about this," Bob concluded, "and I hope we are. But if we're going to face facts, we have to look at the sort of dog Bramble is."

It was all too clear to Neil. He'd only just noticed how powerful Bramble was when Harry Grey had told them he was a German hunting terrier.

"He's bred for hunting," Bob went on, "and he has a strong jaw. That's what they probably want in a fighting dog."

"That's vile," said Harry in a low voice. "Anyone who can take a good dog and turn him into that must be sick." He stood up. "I'd better call the police."

"I'll do it," said Bob. "We're already working together on this."

"Dad," said Neil, "you remember those two brothers who had Bramble in the first place? Carl and Gary?"

"Remember them?" said Bob. "They man-handled

you through the woods and kept you locked up in the old icehouse. I could hardly forget."

"They're banned from keeping dogs, aren't they?" said Neil.

"Banned and fined, and they'd face an even bigger fine if they tried to get away with keeping a dog again," said Bob. "You don't think they've stolen him back, do you?"

"They did once before," Neil reminded him. "They stole him from King Street when we were looking after him. They might have done it again."

"They might, but we've got no evidence," said Bob. "You can't just go blaming people and jumping to conclusions like that, Neil. They don't even live here anymore."

"But they're back! I saw the older brother, Carl, on Compton High Street a few weeks ago. Dad, they were into poaching!" Neil insisted. "It must be them!"

Harry rubbed his chin. "If you remember, Bob, they did set traps at Priorsfield, and my old dog, Mick, got caught," he agreed. "If they're capable of that, they're definitely capable of being part of a dog-fighting ring."

"Yes, they're capable of it, but that doesn't mean they've done it," insisted Bob. "But I am worried about Bramble, so I'm going to call Terri and Sergeant Moorhead. Now, will you walk some of the boarders, Neil? Cassie and Buttons haven't been out yet."

Neil left Harry and his father talking. He picked up a boisterous Jake from the house, then went to the boarding kennel. Soon he was walking Jake with Cassie and Buttons, two of the regular boarders, up to the exercise field, where he let them off their leashes. He knew which dogs could be walked together without fighting. Buttons ran ahead with Jake while Cassie trotted sedately beside him, stopping occasionally to sniff at the grass. Some of the other dogs, mostly males, could be aggressive to each other, growling, snapping, and, if they got the chance, fighting. Neil wondered what happened when that aggressive instinct was trained to turn a well-balanced dog into a brutal fighter.

After the dogs had had a good run, Neil took them back to their kennels, thinking all the time about Titan. If he did survive, what sort of dog would he be? A snarling monster who needed to be muzzled?

He walked back over to the house with Jake and went into the kitchen, where Emily was spreading her homework books across the table.

"I just saw Harry's car leave," she said. "What was that all about?"

Neil immediately told her what had happened and watched her grow white with anger.

"That's horrible!" she said. "How can anyone do that? We've got to do something!"

"I know," muttered Neil, "but we're not supposed to get involved, are we?"

He turned his attention to Sarah, who sat cross-legged on the floor with a piece of straggly knitting that seemed to be getting smaller instead of bigger, and a multicolored heap of wool. Neil watched as Jake leaped onto the pile of wool and tangled it around his snout.

At that moment, Carole Parker came into the room and looked down at the mischievous young dog. "Learning to knit, Jake?" She turned to Neil and Emily. "You two, go and wash your hands before we eat. And Neil, please unwrap Jake first before he strangles himself."

They were clearing up the dinner dishes when the doorbell rang. Neil ran to answer and found Sergeant Moorhead on the doorstep with Terri.

"Is your father at home, Neil?" asked Terri. "We just need to ask him a few more questions."

Neil nodded and showed them through to the office. He waited in the kitchen for them to come out again, and tackled Terri with some questions of his own as soon as they did.

"What's going on?" asked Neil.

"It's not looking good, Neil. This report of Bramble going missing is very disturbing," said Terri sympathetically. "It's too much of a coincidence."

Neil's face fell.

"The good news is that Titan's a little better," said

Terri. "We're on our way to see him. Maybe you two would like to come."

"Definitely!" said Neil. Emily was already on her feet.

"Homework?" said Carole with a raised eyebrow.

"I'll start as soon as I get back. Promise!" said Neil. He and Emily were soon climbing into the SPCA van.

"Have you found out anything more about the dog-fighting ring?" asked Neil as the van drove off.

"You know perfectly well I won't discuss that with you," said Terri firmly, with her eyes on the road. "You don't even know if there is a ring." She remained tight-lipped all the way to the clinic, where Mike came out to meet them.

Neil watched Titan lie dozing in his pen. His head was on his paws, his leg was still bandaged, and the marks of the stitches were clear on his back. Hearing them, Titan raised his head and growled.

"Can he walk yet?" asked Neil.

"He's taken a few steps, but he's still pretty weak," said Mike. "He's done enough for one day, though. I'm going to check up on some of my other in-patients, so I'll leave you with Terri and Sergeant Moorhead."

Titan's persistent growling worried Neil. "He doesn't like us being here," he said. "I think we should go."

"Go out to the van," said Terri, and handed him the

keys. "Wait for me there. I need a word with Sergeant Moorhead."

Neil and Emily went out to the waiting room, and Emily was heading for the door. But Neil lingered just outside the operating room.

"Neil!" whispered Emily, waving for him to join her.

Neil shook his head and put his finger to his lips. He knew that what he was doing was eavesdropping, but he couldn't bear to leave without finding out all he could about Terri's investigation. Emily tiptoed across to stand by him at the door.

"I doubt Carl and Gary Smith are involved," the

policeman was saying. "They're on probation and I doubt they'd want to risk going to jail."

"I'm not so sure, Sergeant," said Terri. "I don't trust them. We should still follow up."

"I suppose."

"I'll visit them at home," said Terri. "If there's any sign of them keeping a dog in the house, we'll have a reason to arrest them because of their ban. I can stop by their place toward the end of the afternoon. Do you know where they're staying?"

"Yes, they had to report to the station last month."

Neil heard the sergeant radioing the station and getting their current address.

"Gary hasn't had a job for a long time," Sergeant Moorhead remarked. "And Carl was employed at an electrical goods warehouse, but he was fired recently. They'll both be in during the day, I suspect."

"OK, I'll see what they're up to," said Terri. "And you might check something out for me."

Neil heard the rustling of papers. He would have given anything to see them.

"Matthew or Matt Jeffrey, also known as Jeffer," she said. "The SPCA is aware of him. He was suspected of involvement in a dogfighting ring near Colshaw, but we didn't have enough evidence for a prosecution. His details and a photograph are in there. I'm wondering if he's still in the area. I'd better go now. It's time I got those kids home."

Neil and Emily dashed for the door. Terri must have stopped to talk a little longer, because they had time to scramble into the van before she appeared. Even so, Neil was sure he looked guilty. Terri seemed to read his thoughts.

"Don't even think of interfering, Neil," she warned as she parked the van at King Street. "I've told you the sort of people we're dealing with here. *Dangerous* people. I'll just pop in and tell your parents how things are."

Neil and Emily jumped out and followed Terri inside.

"I think it's time you did some homework, Neil," was Bob's greeting as they stood in the hallway. "You too, Emily. Do you want to take your books and work in the living room — keep Sarah company?"

Reluctantly, they took the hint and left Terri with Bob and Carole. Jake followed them. At the door, Neil stopped. "You will get Bramble back, won't you? If dogfighting people have got him, you have to find him before they . . ." he didn't even like to say it, "make him fight."

"What do you think I'm here for?" said Terri, arching an eyebrow. Then she smiled warmly. "Don't worry, Neil."

Neil did worry, though. All that evening, whether he was doing homework, watching television, or taking Jake out last thing at night, Bramble was on his mind. He might be a hunting dog and a good ratter, but he wasn't a trained fighter.

As Neil lay in bed, the same pictures turned themselves over and over in his mind. He was haunted by the thought of Bramble locked up and alone, away from his home and his friends. Neil felt pretty sure that Bramble could fight if he had to, but he'd never needed to before now. The idea of Bramble suffering Titan's horrific injuries was unbearable.

Neil heard Bob and Carole lock up the house and go to bed, but he still couldn't sleep. The night seemed to be lasting forever. Talking to somebody about Bramble would help. He got out of bed, slipped on his sweater, and padded across the landing, where a light showed under Emily's door.

"Em?" he whispered, and tapped softly. "Are you still awake?"

When he opened the door, Neil found she was not only awake but out of bed and sitting at her desk in her pajamas and slippers. Neil sat on the bed and curled up to keep warm.

"Can't you sleep, either?" said Emily. "I couldn't bear to think of Bramble ending up like Titan." She took a large sheet of paper she'd been writing on and passed it to him. "I'm making a poster. I've left a space for a photo — I thought we could scan one on the computer."

The word "MISSING" stood out in bold capitals at the top of the poster. Then there was a space for a picture of Bramble, and beneath it the words, "Black-and-tan German hunting terrier. Answers to the name 'Bramble.' Missing from Priorsfield Farm since Monday. Please contact King Street Kennels."

"We'll put the phone number on it," she said, "and we can take posters around to all the usual places. We can even talk to people in the street and ask if they've seen him."

"I suppose so," said Neil, "but if you'd stolen a dog, wouldn't you make sure that nobody saw him?"

"He may not have been stolen, and if he has been they'll want to exercise him to keep him fit for fighting," said Emily.

Neil, thinking about it, had to admit that she was right. "Sergeant Moorhead might not be convinced about Carl and Gary, but I am. I'm sure they're in on this," he said.

"Why?" asked Emily. "Is it one of your famous Neil Parker hunches?"

Neil smiled. "Sort of. But it's more than that, Emily. We know they're back in the area. We know they've got no money coming in because Carl has lost his job."

Emily nodded. "True, so far."

"And we know what they think of dogs," continued Neil. "They have no respect for them. They're cruel and they're prepared to use them to make money."

"They've done it before," added Emily.

"Exactly! I wish we knew where they lived. I know

Terri's checking them out, but I really want to see for myself. This isn't just any dog, it's Bramble."

"Good thing I've got the address."

"You what?" Neil grasped.

"I saw it written in Terri's notebook. She left it open on the dashboard of her van, so I wrote it down as soon as I was in the house. There." She opened her wildlife diary and handed it to him. "126 Prince Albert Terrace."

"How sneaky!" said Neil, but he was smiling. "What about checking it out after school tomorrow?"

"You know what Terri said about staying out of this," Emily reminded him, but he could tell she wasn't convinced.

"Come on, Em," he coaxed. "Why did you write the address down if you didn't mean to do anything about it? Think of Bramble. By this time tomorrow, we might have done something to help him."

"OK," she said. "You're on."

CHAPTER FIVE

After school the next day, Neil and Emily walked to Prince Albert Terrace in Compton. Neil was now beginning to have doubts about what they were doing, but he kept them to himself. Terri had been quite clear in her warning. Dogfighting was a dangerous business run by unscrupulous people. They were supposed to keep out of it. *I must be out of my mind to do this,* he thought. *I need to have my head examined. But it won't do any harm just to take a walk along that way and have a look . . .*

"Em," he said casually, as they turned right at the corner shops, toward Prince Albert Terrace, "there's no need for both of us to go. I'll go on my own and check it out."

"What's the matter with you?" she demanded. "You don't think I'm going home now, do you?"

"I feel as if Bramble's my responsibility. And this was my idea. It might be dangerous."

"Then you need me there to get you out of trouble, don't you? I'm not going home without you. And it was me who took down the address. Either we both go home, or — look, there's Terri's van!"

The white, SPCA van was parked almost at the end of the street. It was empty, so Neil assumed that Terri must be in the house.

"If she sees us, she'll go crazy," said Emily.

"She's not going to see us," said Neil, "not if she's *in* the house. There's a lane over there. It probably leads to the back gates and yards, so let's slip quietly along it and see what we find."

They took the next turn into the back lane and found a low gate with "126" marked on it in crooked white paint. Neil looked at the gate carefully, but there were no telltale canine scratch marks.

"I can't see anyone through the windows," whispered Emily. "They must be talking to Terri at the front of the house, but they could come out at anytime. No sign of a dog, Neil. No barking."

Neil surveyed the yard, but there were no dog toys, no dishes, and no mess. Nothing at all suggested that a dog was being kept there. The yard was, in fact, thoroughly clean and tidy, as if it had just been swept. To the right of the gate, were two brick buildings.

"One of those is a shed, and one's an old coal bunker," said Emily confidently. "All these houses are like that."

"It's all too tidy," murmured Neil. "I don't think Carl and Gary would be that particular about keeping their yard clean. Remember the mess they used to keep the icehouse in? Maybe they're trying to hide something." He leaned over the gate. "I need to look in the outbuildings."

"I'll go," urged Emily. "If they catch me, I'll say I'm — I don't know, looking for my cat, or something, and I might get away with it. You won't. They'll remember you from when they locked you and Chris up in the icehouse."

"Who cares?" said Neil, who was already opening the gate. He was too concerned about Bramble to worry about his own safety. Emily made a face, glanced up at the house to check that all was safe, and followed him.

The first building was padlocked, but there was no door to the old coal bunker. Neil and Emily stepped inside, glad that its shadowy interior would hide them. It was full of cobwebs, with a few old garden tools stacked against the wall, a jacket hanging on a nail, and a broom leaning against a dark corner. Neil, who had hoped to find some evidence of a dog, was disappointed.

"That's the broom they've been sweeping up with," said Emily.

"Any dog hairs on it?" asked Neil.

Emily picked it up. "There isn't even a brush on it!" she said. Neil turned to look. It was only the long wooden handle of a broom, but he snatched at it. He had seen some deep marks in the top, and wanted a better look.

"What is it, Neil?" asked Emily in a whisper.

"Dog tooth marks!" he said in triumph. "I'd know those marks anywhere. We've got our evidence. And look at that jacket!"

"What about it?" she whispered.

With rising excitement, Neil held out the sleeve of the faded coat.

"Dog hairs," said Emily. She picked one up delicately. "Black ones!"

"Yes!" Neil clenched his fist, proud of their success but angry at what it all meant. "They've got Bramble somewhere!"

"Calm down," said Emily, with a glance toward the house. "It doesn't prove anything. It just means that whoever wore this jacket has been in contact with a black dog, or some other animal. And the tooth marks — we don't know . . ."

She stopped suddenly, listening. Then she flattened herself against the sidewall, pushing Neil to do the same. Neil heard the back door of the house opening.

"Give her time to get away." It was a man's gruff

voice, one that Neil would never forget. It was Carl
Smith. "I'll bring the car around the back. Get the
gear out of the shed."

Neil and Emily glanced at each other and pressed
themselves farther into the shadows of the wall.
There was a heavy clump of boots across the yard.
This must be Gary, Carl's younger brother. He wasn't
as smart as Carl, or as ruthless.

The heavy footsteps stopped outside the shed, and
there was a click and snap as the padlock was taken
off. Noiselessly, Neil slipped to the other side of the
bunker. Emily glared at him.

Neil strained for the sound of a whimper, a bark,

or a scrabbling of paws, but all he heard was a rough scraping noise. He sneaked a peak outside. Gary appeared, dragging something that looked like an old cupboard door.

Neil pressed himself back against the wall. The silence made his own breathing seem so loud he felt sure it must be audible.

Gary went away, but was soon back — this time, his brother was with him. Another door was dragged from the shed, then a sheet of corrugated iron.

There was no chance of escaping until the brothers were out of the way. For Neil, that couldn't happen soon enough. The dustiness in the shed made his nose tickle. He tightened his jaw and bit his lip to fight back a sneeze.

Again, Gary and Carl came back. They could see Gary dragging out something that looked like a piece of old garden fence and hauling it to the car, while Carl pulled a cell phone from his pocket and spoke in a low voice. He stood with his back to them, but Neil thought he said something about "Sunday" and "the usual place."

"Seven," finished Carl, and put the phone away. Neil's urge to sneeze subsided. He looked across at Emily. Her eyes were wide with tension and her mouth was set in a tight line.

The back gate banged shut. Neil gave out a long, slow breath. Then he heard Gary's voice.

"We'll need the pole," he called. "It's in the coal bunker. I'll get it."

Sweat broke out across Neil's face. He could hear his heart pounding so loudly he was sure Gary could hear it, too. The footsteps were louder.

"We've got one in the car," shouted Carl. "Come on, let's go."

The footsteps stopped. Gary stood still. Neil held his breath again.

"Do you want your jacket?" called Gary.

"Stop fussing and get in the car!"

Gary's footsteps moved away to the gate. Neil shut his eyes. He shivered.

The car growled away. Without a word, Neil and Emily slipped out of the bunker and through the gate. Then they ran. It had been a lucky escape.

"Where have you been?" demanded Carole sharply as Neil and Emily tumbled breathlessly into the house.

"It's not important," gasped Neil. "We need to see — Terri! You're here!"

"Where you have been is *very* important," said Bob, who was also in the kitchen. "Terri's just here to discuss Titan's future, and she should be off duty by now. I hope you don't intend to keep her waiting any longer. You come in extremely late, looking as if you've been climbing around in an attic somewhere.

We were just about to phone the school and ask if you'd had to stay late. Whatever you've got to tell us, it'd better be good."

"Well," began Neil, "we went home the long way . . ."

"Why?" demanded Carole.

"We just thought we would, and . . ."

Taking turns, with a few pauses and uncertain glances at each other, Neil and Emily told a carefully toned-down version of what they had discovered, and how. When they finished, there was an uncomfortable pause. Terri was stern and tight-lipped.

Bob spoke first. "So you were miles out of your way, and you just happened to wander into Carl and Gary's yard. That's trespassing," he said.

"I don't know why I stay in my job," said Terri sternly. "Why don't I just resign and leave it to you two? You obviously think you can do better than I can."

Neil looked at the floor. "Sorry," he said, "but . . ."

"But nothing, Neil," said Bob. "I know you were only thinking about the welfare of a dog. But do you think Terri doesn't care? I hope you realize that you could have wrecked her whole operation."

"It was me more than Emily," said Neil, ignoring Emily's protests. "We couldn't just stand back and let Bramble be mauled like Titan was."

"Your information *is* useful," admitted Terri, "but

the police and I would have found it out ourselves in time. I was very suspicious about the place being so tidy, so I had a good look around and found some dog hairs. Sergeant Moorhead is going to keep an eye on Carl and Gary. But if they've got Bramble, they're definitely keeping him somewhere else."

"Why were they taking those doors and things out?" asked Emily.

"They use them for setting up the dogfighting arena," said Terri. "They call it a ring, but it's more or less square, like a boxing ring. They put the dogs in there to fight."

"And the pole?" asked Emily.

"That's used to teach the dogs to grip with their teeth. The owners make a game of it. They hold the pole and shake it while the dog bites the other end. It's to strengthen the jaw and encourage them to grip and hang on."

"Everybody plays with dogs like that," Emily pointed out. "You use a soft toy or a dog pull or something."

"Yes," said Terri, "but when these people do it, they're training the dogs to treat another animal like that. And yes, I know it's horrible," she went on as she saw the disgust on Emily's face, "but if you insist on involving yourselves in my cases, you have to face unpleasant facts."

"Neil, are you listening to this?" asked Carole sternly.

"They definitely said, 'Sunday,'" he told Terri. "And I think it was 'seven.'"

"That's worth knowing," said Terri, "if they're organizing a fight. But he could have been arranging to meet a friend, for all we know. And if it's a fight, we don't know where."

The doorbell rang, and Carole went to answer it. Neil heard her talking to a visiting customer, and eventually Bob went to join her. Left with Emily and Terri, Neil suddenly said, "I've got it!"

"Got what," said Emily.

"The 'usual place.' Remember the icehouse at Priorsfield Farm?"

"Icehouse?" asked Terri.

"It's like a walk-in freezer built into the ground," explained Neil, "from the days when they didn't have fridges. It's secluded and just about soundproof, and they've used it before. I think that might be it!"

"Could be," agreed Terri. "But it won't be very big. I'll see what Sergeant Moorhead says."

"I don't understand," said Emily. "You don't need to know where the fight's taking place, because you're not going to let it happen, are you? Can't you just arrest Carl and Gary now?"

"Emily," said Terri. "At the moment, we haven't got any evidence. We don't even know if Titan was used in a dogfight — and Bramble *could* have just run away. The police and I have to keep a low profile and let them meet for the dogfight."

"But . . ." began Emily.

"Then we swoop," said Terri. "Before any dog can be hurt. The timing has to be perfect, and we don't need anyone to mess it up for us. Got it?"

Neil nodded. He didn't feel he had a choice.

CHAPTER SIX

Neil and Emily were eating breakfast the next morning when Bob answered the door to find Sergeant Moorhead. There was some quiet conversation on the doorstep, then the tall policeman strode into the kitchen.

"I'm paying an early call to Mike's clinic, to take a look at the evidence," he said. "I believe the evidence is wagging its tail and eating everything Mike puts in front of it. He's making excellent progress, and I thought you'd like to see him again. Want to come along?"

Neil jumped to his feet, nearly tripping over a bundle of pink wool that Jake had unraveled across the floor. "Titan!" he exclaimed. "Is he going to be all right?"

"Come and see him for yourself," said Sergeant Moorhead, "and then I'll drop you off at school. Mike thinks the dog's well enough to have visitors."

Neil and Emily fell over each other to get their books packed, and hurried out to the gleaming white police van. Sherlock, Sergeant Moorhead's young German shepherd, barked a greeting to them from behind the grille.

"You know the old guy who works as Harry Grey's shepherd?" said Sergeant Moorhead as he drove. "Nick Christmas — or whatever his name is. Did he say anything when the dog was found? Did he react in any way?"

"I think he was as upset as everyone else," said Emily.

"He was sort of muttering to himself when we left," remembered Neil.

"I see." Sergeant Moorhead was thoughtful. "Might be worth having a word with old Father Christmas. He might know something. He's been wandering around these parts long enough to have a few country-side connections. Here we are. Mike's expecting us."

Mike Turner appeared from a side door and beck-oned them all around to a small yard at the back of the clinic. But when Neil put out a hand to open the gate, Mike stopped him.

"I'm going to bring Titan out here," he said. "But this is just so you can see him, not approach him. I don't know what he's going to be like with strangers, and I don't intend to find out the hard way. Staffies can be tough little customers, even without Titan's bad experiences."

He left them there while he walked across the yard to the back door of the clinic. Soon there was an uneven padding of paws, and Titan appeared.

Compared with his appearance on Saturday, Neil thought Titan looked great. Pale pink skin still showed through the smooth coat where Mike had needed to shave him for his operation, and there were scabs where the wounds were knitting together in deep, dark lines. Neil could see immediately that the dog was out of danger. Titan walked slowly, limping from the injury to his right foreleg, but he planted himself firmly in the middle of the yard and barked hoarsely at them.

"He looks like he's over the worst," said Neil. "What happens to him now?"

"Officially, he's still in the care of the police," said Mike, "but in the meantime, I'm hoping you can find him a place at King Street. He may be a rescue dog, but you won't be able to send him to a new home until the case is over."

Titan, still barking, made a stiff and awkward run at the gate.

"The trouble is, I don't know if he can be placed," Mike went on as he watched the terrier hobbling about. "He'll never be a family dog. He comes from an aggressive breed and he's been trained to fight — to attack and hold on, and not think too hard about it first. Not your average cuddly pet for children. We'll need to be sure about any danger he might pose before he goes anywhere."

"He has to find a home somewhere," insisted Emily. "If he can't live with a family, he might make a good companion for someone lonely."

"We'll have to wait and see," said Mike. "He did a lot of growling at Janice and me early on, but I can't blame him for that. No dog likes the vet. He's all right with us now, but I haven't tried him with anyone else. If he's always been a fighting dog and never learned to behave himself, frankly, his chances aren't good."

"But then he'd have to be —" began Neil.

"Destroyed, yes," said Mike. "Like Duke, that dog you had once at the kennel, remember? He bit everyone who got close enough, including your mom."

"Is Titan really like that?" asked Emily.

"I hope not. I haven't gone to all this trouble making him better just to put him to sleep. If he shows that he can behave like a reasonably civilized sort of dog, he'll get a home with somebody. He'll always be lame, though. There was a lot of damage to the tendons in the right foreleg. Tell you what — I wouldn't like to meet the dog he was up against."

"Neither would Bramble," said Emily under her breath. She turned away from the yard, and Neil saw the worry on her face.

"I'd better take you two to school now," said Sergeant Moorhead. "And, Mike, d'you think you'll be available on Sunday night?"

He was about to say more, but, glancing at Neil and Emily, he stopped himself. "Hop in the car, you two," he said. "I'll be there in a minute."

They strapped themselves into the car and waited until he had finished talking to Mike. Neil turned to pet Sherlock through the grille.

"They must be arranging something for Sunday,"

said Emily. "But that's far off. Almost four days. It's a long time for Bramble to be with those people — if he has been stolen for a fight."

"You said yourself, dogfighting men would want to keep their dogs fit," said Neil. "They won't let him go hungry or anything." Sherlock's ears lifted as Sergeant Moorhead came back to the car.

"They better not let anything happen to him," muttered Emily. "They better not."

That night, Neil and Emily scanned their "Missing Dog" poster into the computer. Neil found a picture of Bramble in their files, scanned it, and set it under the words "Have you seen this dog?"

"Make sure you put the phone number," said Bob, watching them work, "so that anyone who has information can contact us immediately. Where are you taking the posters?"

"The usual places — the police station, Mike's clinic, Meadowbank School, Mrs. Smedley's, newsstands, and so on," said Neil. "And we can approach people in the street as well, show them the poster, and ask if they've seen him."

"Just as long as you don't make total nuisances of yourselves," said Bob, and smiled as Sarah appeared. She held up something small, yellow, and woolly that looked like a bird's nest.

"My first blanket!" she said proudly.

"Oh, that's beautiful, Sarah!" said Bob.

"Very good," said Emily, and nudged Neil.

"Wonderful," said Neil. "Who's it for?"

"Bramble," she said. "For when you find him."

Neil was desperate to take the posters out as soon as they were ready on Friday evening, but Carole persuaded him to wait. There would be a lot more people shopping on High Street the next morning.

On Saturday, Emily and Neil biked to the center of Compton. They patrolled High Street, asking shop-keepers to put up posters and handing over pictures to people at bus stops and passers-by in the street. By the middle of the morning they had very few posters left, but also no definite leads. They stopped to buy sodas at Mrs. Smedley's shop and sat on a nearby bench to drink them.

"I had one lady say she saw a dog a little like him on a leash in the park on Wednesday," said Neil. "But I don't think you'd walk a stolen dog where everyone could see him."

"And I met a boy who was sure he'd seen him, but that was last Sunday, before he was dognapped," said Emily. She stared thoughtfully at the half-empty soda can. "Maybe we're looking in the wrong places."

Neil was about to ask what she meant, then he realized it for himself. "You mean, we should be over at the Prince Albert Terrace end of town where Carl and Gary live?" he said.

Emily nodded.

"I agree," said Neil, "but if we're seen around there with posters, Carl and Gary might hear about it and know that we're on to them."

"Isn't Bramble worth the risk?" suggested Emily.

"Let's go for it, then," he said.

They unlocked their bikes and rode to the corner of Prince Albert Terrace. Apart from the woman in the corner shop and two of Neil and Emily's school friends waiting for a bus, there was hardly anyone around. They chained their bikes to a railing and hovered outside the shop, wondering where to put up their posters.

"Let's start with the bus stop," said Neil. "We could talk to people as they're getting off buses, too. Come on, let's take a walk down the street until the next bus gets here."

They wandered down the road that ran at right angles to Prince Albert Terrace. It was a long street, leading to a children's playground and, beyond that, a footpath to the park. It was growing cool. Neil hunched his shoulders and pushed his hands into his pockets as they walked past a blue van.

Something caught his eye. He stopped and turned around.

"What is it?" said Emily.

Neil had returned to the rear of the van. "Emily!" he said. "Look at this!"

Emily was beside him. Hanging across the rear windows of the van was an old and shabby curtain.

"That's Titan's curtain!" said Emily. "The one he was found wrapped up in!"

It was unmistakable. The same off-white background and purple flowers. Neil tapped on the window.

"Bramble?" he said hopefully.

Emily turned away to keep watch as Neil listened intently at the back of the van. But there wasn't a sound.

"There's no dog in there," said Neil at last. "But we do know there's a connection between this van and Titan. We'll have to remember the license plate number."

Emily took a pen from her pocket and wrote the number on the back of her hand, occasionally glancing around.

"Should we call Sergeant Moorhead?" suggested Emily.

"No, the best thing to do," said Neil, "is to wait and see who comes for the van."

"But we shouldn't be seen," said Emily. "And they might not come back until — oh! Neil, look! Quick!"

A big man with wild, straggly hair was walking along the footpath in the park a few hundred yards away, clearly silhouetted for a moment against the skyline. They saw him jerk at an extending leash. A dark shape scampered toward him.

"Bramble!" Neil ran for his bike with Emily following. "Quick!" he yelled over his shoulder.

They pedaled the rest of the length of Prince Albert Terrace and tore along the first fifty yards of the footpath. Breathless already, they abandoned their bikes as the path became too uneven to navigate speedily, and ran.

As they ran up the hill, rain was beginning to fall and the sky was heavy. Squinting against it as he ran, Neil saw no sign of man or dog, though he yelled Bramble's name until his throat and lungs hurt. He struggled farther up the steep path, searching one way and then the other, until at last, wet and gasping for breath, he knew it was no good. Kicking angrily at pebbles, he stumbled back with Emily to where they had left their bikes.

"The bike seats are soaked," Emily said, wiping them with her sleeve. "Let's go home and get dry."

"We need to tell Terri and Sergeant Moorhead," Neil said as he climbed onto his bike. "We need to tell them about the van. And that we think we saw Bramble — but managed to lose him again," he added grimly.

He got on his bike and started pedaling, not talking to Emily on the journey home. They had been so close to Bramble, but they had not been fast enough. They had let him down.

CHAPTER SEVEN

Neil felt a bit better once he had been welcomed home by Jake and changed into dry clothes. When their information had been passed on to Terri and Sergeant Moorhead, Neil and Emily sat down to bowls of hot tomato soup and Neil realized how much he needed it. He was halfway through his second helping when an idea struck him.

"Can we go to Priorsfield this afternoon?" he suggested.

"Who's 'we'?" asked Carole.

"Well, me — and Em, if she wants to come," he added, looking across at his sister. "Anyone else?"

"Me!" said Sarah, bouncing on her seat. "I can see my lamb. And show Mrs. Grey my knitting."

"I'll drop you all off," said Carole, "but you'll have to check with the Greys that it's OK. And, remember, you two are responsible for Sarah. Also, you're to stay around the farm buildings and the lambing shed — you're not to go into the woods if there are dangerous people hanging around Priorsfield. You are *not* there to do Terri's job. I want your solemn promise on this."

"Promise," said Neil and Emily together, knowing they didn't have any alternative.

At Priorsfield Farm, Mrs. Grey admired Sarah's latest attempt at knitting and then led her off to see the lambs. Sarah's namesake was tucked under the mother ewe, her head tilted as she suckled.

Neil and Emily found Harry Grey in the tractor shed with Tuff, who ran to meet them before hurtling off to attack a bit of twine that was blowing in the breeze.

They told Harry about their morning's work. When they came to their sighting of Bramble, he grew sharp-eyed and attentive. "You're sure it was him? Absolutely sure?"

"I didn't see him for long, but it was long enough," said Neil. "I'm sure it was Bramble. I'm sorry we couldn't get him back for you."

"I don't suppose you recognized the man, did you?"

Neil shook his head. "I don't think it was Carl or

Gary. Carl's quite gangly and Gary is quite short. This man was pretty hefty, with frizzy hair. Oh, hi, Nick!"

Nick Christmas was ambling toward them. He gave a nod in their direction, but turned his attention to Harry. "Have you used that corrugated iron? I had it stacked behind the kennel, and it isn't there now."

"I haven't touched it," said Harry. "What was it for?"

"Pens. I was going to make pens for the lambs, but it's gone."

Neil and Emily exchanged glances, then Neil told Harry all they had seen at Carl and Gary's house, and what Terri had told them about dogfighting.

"We've told Terri and the police everything," Emily assured him, as Neil told Nick about their sighting of Bramble.

"Big man?" he said, narrowing his eyes. "You say a big man had him? How big? What did he look like? Did he have spiky, wild-looking hair?"

"Yes, I think so," said Neil.

Harry looked sharply at him. "Why, Nick? Do you think you might know him?"

Nick glanced at him, then at Neil. "Could be Jeffer," he said in a low voice.

"Jeffer?" said Neil. He remembered Terri mentioning that name. He was about to say so, but he caught sight of Emily shaking her head at him. He guessed what she was thinking, and she was right. If Nick thought he might end up in trouble with the SPCA and the law, he wouldn't tell them anything.

"Who's Jeffer?" asked Emily innocently.

Nick shrugged. "I met him in a diner a few weeks back. He asked me about the lambing and that."

"And that?" said Harry Grey. "What's 'and that' supposed to mean?"

"Please, Nick," implored Emily, "please, if you know anything, tell us. You won't get into any trouble. We don't want Bramble to be hurt, that's all."

"He asked me where I worked and what it was like," said Nick.

"And about dogs?" asked Neil.

"Yes. And about dogs." Nick shifted from one foot to the other.

"Was he with anyone?" asked Emily.

"Not when I saw him," admitted Nick. "But as I was going *into* the diner . . ." Nick hesitated, "that Carl Smith was just coming *out.*"

Neil and Emily exchanged incredulous looks.

"Now I'm off," said Nick. "I've got lambs to look after."

"That's it!" said Neil as Nick shambled away out of earshot. "Terri said there was a local man called Jeffer who's been involved in dogfighting before, and they think he might be connected with this case. Being in the same diner as Carl Smith is too much of a coincidence for it not to mean something."

"You might be right, Neil," said Harry. "It does seem hard to believe they're not colluding in some way, what with their past histories. We'd better let Terri know what Nick's told us. I'll give her a call." He strode purposefully into the house.

Neil and Emily leaned against a fence and sighed. "At last we're getting somewhere," said Neil. He clenched his fist in triumph.

Their attention was caught by Tuff as he did a little patrol of the farmyard.

Emily looked around. "Those little ducklings are getting adventurous," she said. "Look, they're coming toward the gate. Aren't they sweet? I wonder if they think we're going to feed them."

Three tawny-yellow ducklings with downy feathers pattered away from the duck pond, their mother behind them. They waddled busily toward the house and slipped beneath some loose netting hanging underneath the gate.

There was a sharp growl from Tuff and a gasp from Neil as he tried to grab the terrier. But it was too late. Tuff galloped across the farmyard to the ducklings, ignoring all commands, barking and snapping as Neil and Emily ran after him. Emily snatched up the nearest duckling, but the others stayed still, unaware of the danger.

"Tuff! No!" yelled Neil, but Tuff was almost on top of the nearest helpless ducklings.

The sound of strong wings beating above them made them look up. With a powerful rush an adult duck swept down on Tuff, pecking in fury. In the moment that it took Tuff to dodge and look for his attacker, Neil and Emily had rescued the ducklings and shooed them back under the gate.

"Quick, get away before the mother duck goes for us, too," said Emily breathlessly.

"I don't think she will," said Neil. "I think she knows the difference between us and a Jack Russell."

"But a Jack Russell can't tell a duckling from a rat," said Emily. She pushed her hair out of her eyes and watched anxiously as the ducklings scurried back to their pond. "Sometimes I wonder if dogs really are that intelligent."

"Good save, you!" Harry Grey was coming out of the farmhouse. "I saw that from the window! I'll have to nail some wire mesh on that gate — the ducklings are getting more adventurous."

"Perhaps Tuff's bored," said Emily. "He's got no-body to play with now."

"He's been fidgety ever since Bramble disappeared," agreed Harry. "I've just had a word with Terri. She thinks the corrugated iron, Bramble, the Smith brothers, and this Jeffer guy are all connected. And all part of this dogfighting racket."

"I knew it!" said Neil.

Harry Grey grinned. "Guesses are one thing. Evidence is another. From what she said, I understand they're planning to stake out the old icehouse on Sunday night — oops!" He looked almost guilty. "I should have kept my big mouth shut. I don't think I was supposed to tell you that."

"That's all right." Emily smiled. "We don't mind."

On Sunday evening, Bob and Bev, who were on weekend duty, had finished the walking, watering, and feeding of the dogs. In the Parkers' living room, Sarah was busy with her knitting. Carole had gone out to see her brother Jack in town.

"Dad," said Neil suddenly, glancing up from the TV. "Can I take Jake for a long walk?"

Bob looked surprised to be asked. "Of course you can," he said.

Neil crossed his fingers. "To Priorsfield?" he asked.

Bob looked out the window. "Be back before it gets dark," he said. "By eight o'clock."

"Don't worry," said Emily, closing the book she had been reading. "I'll go with him and hold his hand."

Neil and Emily left Bob reading Sarah a story.

Priorsfield was a long walk away, but it was a nice evening and Jake was enjoying the exercise. Instead of heading for the farmhouse, Neil took the road which led past a few cottages to the woods.

Neil felt a bit guilty about having misled his father about why he was going out, but Bramble's safety was too important. "The icehouse is this side of the woods," he told Emily.

"I expected to see some police cars," said Emily. "Maybe they're keeping a low profile."

"Maybe," mumbled Neil.

Neil whistled to Jake, who wheeled away from the tree he was sniffing and trotted obediently back to them. Neil clipped on his leash. It was very quiet, with an uneasy stillness in the air.

"Let's wait up here," Emily whispered to Neil, pointing to a patch of bare ground on the hillside, partly screened by trees. "They're supposed to meet at seven, and it's twenty to. We'll have a good view of the icehouse here."

"Can you see the door in the hillside?" asked Neil.

"Yes," said Emily, narrowing her eyes and following the direction of his arm. "But I can't see any of the police, or Terri. They must be here somewhere, right?"

"Of course they're here," said Neil, hoping he sounded more positive than he felt. The idea of meeting a whole gang of dogfighting men in the woods with only Jake to protect them wasn't something that filled him with confidence.

Minutes ticked away. Now and then Neil or Emily would creep a little way down the hillside or back to the path, but there was no sign of anyone coming. Jake sniffed the air, ears twitching.

"Perhaps we've got it all wrong," said Emily. "The wrong Sunday, or something. It'll be dark soon. D'you think we should go home?"

"I'll go and do one last check," said Neil. "I won't go far. I'll take Jake."

With Jake close at his heel, he crept along the hill in the unnatural quietness, noticing for the first time that dusk was falling.

In the undergrowth below the icehouse, something moved, but he couldn't tell who or what. Riveted, he watched the spot. He was watching so carefully that he heard nothing until Jake sat up and growled.

The hair prickled on the back of his neck. With one hand on Jake's collar, he turned.

"Neil Parker," said a familiar voice. "I might have known."

CHAPTER EIGHT

The fear that had crept through Neil gave way to joyous relief.

"Terri!" he gasped, and put out a hand to quiet Jake.

Terri was standing behind him holding a radio. Her face was stern and her eyes furious. "Neil Parker, you are a menace to us all!" she hissed. She crouched down and motioned to him to do the same. "What are you up to? Are you here alone?"

"Emily's over there," he said. "Near the gate."

"And you left her there, knowing the sort of people who might be in the woods! You do know what's going on, don't you? That's why you're here! I don't suppose your parents know where you are, do they?"

"Yes," said Neil cautiously.

"You mean, yes, but if they'd known we were staking out the woods they'd never have let you come anywhere near here," she said angrily. She scanned the woods, narrowing her eyes as she peered into the fading light, then waved. Emily crept to her side from her hiding place several yards away. She moved as softly as she could, trying to avoid fallen twigs that cracked underfoot.

"Do you want to let the whole world know we're here?" demanded Terri in a low, angry voice. "This is ridiculous. The police and I have planned this operation to the last detail, and you come crashing through like an army."

"Sorry," whispered Neil and Emily in turn.

"I hope you are," Terri went on. "There are police throughout these woods. We're holding on to give the fighting ring a chance to meet at the icehouse and get the fight set up."

"But —" began Emily. Terri silenced her with a look.

"We have to move in when they're ready to fight, so we have evidence and witnesses. The timing has to be perfect. And we really don't need you tagging along."

Neil glanced at Emily. "Perhaps we should go," he said reluctantly, but that only made it worse.

"I can't leave you wandering around here now!" scolded Terri. "You're enough trouble already without blundering around in the dark. And there are ruthless people nearby. We can't spare anyone to escort you or be a baby-sitter."

"But we can take care of ourselves!" argued Neil.

"Shut up and do as you're told for once. Stay by me, keep down, and don't make a sound."

They crouched down as low as they could, in the hope that they would not be seen. Slowly, unbearably slowly, the time passed. Every rustle and every gust of wind in the trees made their spines tingle, but nobody appeared.

Terri pressed a button on her radio and spoke softly. They heard the responding voice of Sergeant Moorhead from his hiding place somewhere in the woods.

"Nothing happening here, Terri. How about you?"

"Nothing," she answered. "Have we got the wrong Sunday? Or the wrong time? Could they have duped us?"

"Impossible to tell. We'll stay put for now."

"And," added Terri, "could you radio one of the officers in the cars to phone King Street Kennels, please?" She gave the number and glanced at Neil and Emily. "Tell Bob Parker that Neil and Emily are with me. And that they're safe."

She switched off the radio. "Safe, but only because I'm not allowed to spank the pair of you," she said. "Now all we can do is be patient."

"But what if we're waiting in the wrong place?" Emily asked. "Right night, right time, wrong place?"

"Quite possible," muttered Terri.

"But then it could already be happening, some-where else!" Emily whispered. "We're all hanging around here while they're probably somewhere else, setting a monster dog on Bramble!"

Neil, with one hand on Jake's collar, looked over at Terri and saw that she was uneasy. He struggled to make sense of all he'd learned over the last week. A thought suddenly began to form in Neil's head. "Em," he said at last, "didn't Sergeant Moorhead say Carl had been fired from a warehouse recently?"

"A warehouse?" Suddenly, Terri looked bright again. "Yes, I was there when he said that. A warehouse would be just the sort of place for a dogfight."

"Which one did he work at, though?" said Neil. "It could be anywhere. Do you know?"

"No," said Terri, "but I'm sure Sergeant Moorhead does." She switched on the radio and whispered urgently.

Ten minutes later they were in her van, racing to Colshaw Road, hoping they would be in time to stop Bramble from getting seriously injured. Terri had radioed her intentions to Sergeant Moorhead immediately, and all of the local police involved in the operation were converging on their new destination.

"It's an electrical goods warehouse next to the crafts store," explained Terri as she drove. "My guess is that Carl had a set of keys copied. And there are no houses along there, so nobody would notice people turning up on a Sunday evening."

Neil looked in the rearview mirror. "I thought the police were coming with us," he said. "I can't see them."

Terri looked in the mirror, too. "Look again," she said.

"I can see a red Sierra," said Neil. "Oh, and Mike Turner's in the passenger seat!"

"We thought we'd better bring him along," said Terri. "And the driver is a policeman in plain clothes. That's an unmarked police car. The others are coming by a different route, so we don't look conspicuous and give ourselves away. Emily, will you stop looking at the clock!"

"I can't help it," she complained. "I'm afraid we'll be too late."

"There's not a thing I can do about that," said Terri brusquely.

The next set of traffic lights turned red as they approached them, and Neil saw Emily begin to chew her nails. He found his own hands were clenched into white-knuckled fists. Jake, at his feet, glanced from one side to the other, aware of the tension around him, his ears pricked up and twitching. The traffic lights seemed to be taking much longer than usual to change. At last Terri turned right and gathered speed along the wide, straight road.

Suddenly, she braked so sharply that Neil and

Emily were flung forward against their seat belts before they could see what was happening. Neil grabbed Jake, who was scrabbling to find his balance, and the horn sounded its strident warning.

"That's all we need!" muttered Terri angrily. Neil opened his eyes.

A wiry young man wearing jeans and a parka stood in the road in front of them. Neil saw the wildly waving arms and the helpless distress on the lean face.

"That's Gary Smith!" he cried.

Neil, Terri, and Emily jumped from the van. Gary ran to Terri and started to tell her something, but his words were confused and rushed, and made no sense.

The red Sierra pulled up to the curb behind them. Mike and the police officer scrambled out.

"Calm down, Gary," Terri was saying. "Catch your breath. Now, try again. What are you trying to tell me?"

"They've got my dog! My dog!" he exclaimed. "You've got to get him back!"

"Bramble?" demanded Emily.

"Jack!" blurted Gary desperately. "They've got Jack!"

"That's Bramble," said Neil, remembering that Carl and Gary had called him Jack. "Are they at the warehouse?"

"Have they started fighting?" asked Emily.

"Yes — no — I don't know." Gary struggled to make sense. "They're all in there — Carl and all of them — and he's got Bully." Puzzled, he looked at Neil. "You're that dog boy, aren't you? Can you help me get my dog back?"

"Get in the van," ordered Terri, and they obeyed her quickly. "Who's Bully?" she asked as they drove away.

"Carl's dog. A pit bull. He's so mean," stammered Gary nervously. "Carl got him for fighting." His face was haggard with anxiety.

"How did you know we were coming?" asked Terri.

"I didn't. I just wanted anyone to stop and help. Didn't care who. Carl said it was all right. He said the dogs like fighting."

"Like it!" Neil's rage exploded as he turned on Gary. "Being torn to pieces? Would you like it?"

Gary wriggled uneasily. "I tried to save the last one," he said. "I wrapped him up. I left him at the farm."

"Quiet, everyone," said Terri. "We're here. I'll park on a side street, in case there are lookouts. Gary, we need to get inside the warehouse without being seen. If they know we're here, they'll all be out a back entrance like a bunch of scared rabbits. Can you help us?"

"Carl usually goes in and out through the side doors," said Gary, "but he's also got an escape route. You go across the yard and down the steps into the boiler room."

"Show me," said Terri quickly. Alert and ready for action, she seemed to have forgotten Neil and Emily as they scrambled from the van. Neil didn't like leaving Jake behind, but he didn't dare take him, either. He shut the door, taking care to leave a window open a few inches. Just then, a marked police car appeared from the opposite direction. Seconds later, Mike Turner arrived in his unmarked car with another police officer.

"Cover the side doors," the SPCA officer said into her radio. "And any fire exits. And the boiler room entrance, which is where I'm going. Gary, show me the way."

Quickly and quietly, she and Gary ran across the

yard. Neil and Emily followed. Neil saw a row of dumpsters and a low, flat-roofed shed next to the warehouse wall. Beside the shed, there was a flight of steps. Terri led the way as they ran down the steps and into the boiler room. It was almost empty except for a water tank in one corner. A blue-painted door with a mesh-covered window overlooked the adjoining room.

Gary nodded at the door. "In there," he whispered. His hands were twisting and fidgeting with agitation.

"There's no noise," Neil whispered to Emily. "No barking, no shouting, no anything. They must not have started yet."

"Or else it's already over, and we've come too late," said Emily. Her face was white and her eyes wide.

Silent as a mouse, Terri slipped over to the window and looked into the next room. Neil and Emily crept to the door and stood pressed together, shoulder to shoulder. Hardly daring to breathe and afraid of what they might see, they looked through the mesh into the place where, at any minute, Bramble might have to fight for his life — or where, if they were too late, he might already be abandoned and dying.

CHAPTER NINE

Through the mesh window Neil saw a very mixed crowd of people, mostly men, but with a few women among them. Some were casually dressed but others wore suits and ties, as if this was an important occasion and they had dressed up for it. On a table were bottles and cans of beverages. Evidently, a dog-fight was considered a good night out by some people.

Neil caught sight of the doors and corrugated iron he had seen Carl and Gary putting into their car, and he felt slightly sick when he saw how they were being used. They had been made into a makeshift enclosure in the middle of the room. There was a thick layer of clean sawdust in the center, with a line drawn across it.

He reassured himself that if the sawdust was clean, no fighting could have taken place yet. The thought of dogs being set to fight each other had been bad enough, but to be there when it was about to happen was worse. He would never understand how these people could find dogfighting so entertaining.

However, although he leaned to one side and then the other to get a better view, he could see no sign at all of Bramble. In fact, there were no dogs at all. That, at least, was a relief.

Just then, two of the men in suits dragged out folding tables from somewhere and set them up beside the fighting ring. They looked like they were there for a purpose, and Neil wondered what that was. He felt there was something menacing about the two empty tabletops.

He heard a door opening. Two more men strode into view.

First came Carl, one hand waving to the crowd like a sports star, the other hanging on tightly to a short leash. The dog on the leash was heavily boned and muscular, with powerful shoulders and a pronounced jaw. Neil was glad it wore a muzzle. Behind Carl came a man Neil had seen only once before, at a distance in the park, but he remembered the bulky figure and wild hair. Somebody called out, "Nice dog, Jeffer!" Then Neil saw the dog, and his heartbeat quickened.

It was Bramble. And he was wearing a muzzle!

Bramble must be hating it. He walked at the man's heel on a short, tight leash, but there was no lightness or spring in his step. The two men stopped beside the ring, bent to pick up their dogs, and hoisted them onto the tables.

There was a bustle of movement as everyone gathered round to take a good look at the two dogs. Neil could hear questions being asked about their weight and their history.

"Bully's a great fighter," said one of the men, admiring Carl's dog. "I saw him in action once. He never lets go. He nearly finished Rambo."

"What happened to Rambo?" asked somebody else.

"I told Gary to finish him off and dump him in a garbage can somewhere," said Carl. "He wasn't going to live through the night."

"Where's Gary tonight?" somebody asked.

"Dunno." Carl looked around the room. Neil froze, terrified at the idea of meeting those searching eyes. "Gone for some food, I suppose. He doesn't have the stomach for this game. He's a wimp, that's what he is."

Neil glanced over his shoulder and saw Gary retreat into a shadowy corner, trembling at the sound of his own brother's voice.

Neil's palms were clammy. If they wondered where Gary was . . . If they guessed that he might have gone to find help . . . But nobody showed any more interest in his whereabouts. The coming fight was far more important to them. Neil looked back at the fight scene through the window.

"Bully's in good shape," said Carl.

Jeffer ran his hand along Bully's solid back. "I'll put a thousand on him," he said.

Soon, there was a businesslike hum of organization while the crowd placed bets. Neil heard snatches of their conversation. "The new dog's leaner and fitter . . ." "Yes, but it's his first fight. Bully knows the score . . ." "Where'd you get him, Jeffer? Oh, I see. Better not to ask. Let's have a look at his teeth."

Neil saw Emily turn her head just enough to send Terri an imploring glance.

Terri, watching intently, shook her head. "Not yet," she whispered. "Just a few seconds longer."

The press of people around the dogs obscured Neil's view. Irritated, he stretched up to see, but it was useless. Then he heard a loud, commanding voice that he felt sure must be Jeffer's.

"Stand back, ladies and gentlemen, for your own safety, while we remove the muzzles."

The crowd parted and stood back. Jeffer and Carl unfastened the muzzles from the dogs' jaws.

"Beautiful jaw on this dog," said Carl, showing off the pit bull's head. "Do you want to see his teeth?"

"Just look at this," said Jeffer. "This is a class dog. Look at —"

There was a loud and rising snarl from Carl's dog.

The crowd gasped. With snapping teeth, the pit bull hurled itself at Bramble.

Emily shrieked, "No!"

The murmuring around the tables stopped as Carl dragged his dog away and all heads turned to the door. On the other side, Terri backed away, firing rapid commands into her radio. For a moment, Jeffer looked wildly from side to side. He watched the crush of bodies heading for the fire exit, then he let go of Bramble and, with heavy determination, ran directly for the boiler room door. Into the radio, Terri ordered, *"Now!"*

Jeffer burst through the door with such force that Neil and Emily were flung against the wall and fell to the floor. He bolted for the steps, but in his way stood Terri, still clutching her radio.

For a terrible moment, it seemed as if he would charge straight at the steps and force her out of his way, but he obviously saw something that stopped him.

Two uniformed policemen appeared at the top of the stairs. Stepping out of the shadows to Jeffer's right, Gary moved forward and glared at the man who had been about to put his old dog Bramble into the ring with a vicious killer.

Jeffer caught his eye, sneered, then turned and ran back into the room toward the fire doors, where the rest of the ring were pushing each other aside to get out. Carl was among them, dragging Bully roughly on his leash. Bramble, abandoned and afraid, ran backward and forward, barking frantically.

"Bramble!" yelled Neil as he and Emily picked themselves up from the floor, and together they sprinted into the now empty room. Bramble heard Neil's voice and ran toward him, but somebody else, loping past Neil, reached the dog first.

In a second, Gary was kneeling on the floor. He held Bramble tightly in his arms. "It's all right now," he was saying. "I've got you. Nobody's going to hurt you. It's all right."

Neil sat on the floor beside them, keeping a cautious distance from Bramble. However much he cared for the dog, he wondered how much Jeffer might have done to bring out aggression and violence in him. Bramble wriggled free from Gary's arms and backed away, crouching and growling.

"What's the matter with him?" Gary asked Neil.

"He's probably scared to death," said Neil.

"But he's the best dog," said Gary. "He's just great. I never wanted Jeffer to get him. He was happy where he was, on his farm, weren't you, Jack — I mean, what do you call him?"

"Bramble," said Emily. "His name's Bramble."

"You won't be able to keep him," said Neil, anxiously watching Bramble. "You understand that, don't you?"

Gary nodded and stroked Bramble's head. The dog growled a little. "He should go back to his farm," he said. "He liked it there."

Neil stood up. "Let's see what's going on," he said.

They found Bramble's leash, and Neil very carefully fastened it on and took him back through the boiler room, up the steps, and into the yard. The evening was colder now, and darker. Several people were being led to police cars, where an officer held Sherlock beside him. Carl, with Bully held close on his leash, stood flanked by two policemen as Sergeant Moorhead strode toward him.

"It'll be all right now," said Neil to Emily. "It's all under —"

He never finished. With a word and a quick movement, Carl had slipped off Bully's leash. Snarling, the powerful dog launched himself forward, but, even as Sergeant Moorhead sidestepped, it was clear that Bully was not going to attack him. He had been trained to attack dogs, not people, and he was aiming for Bramble's throat.

Neil caught Bramble up in his arms, but he knew he couldn't outrun the pit bull. He heard Jake's frantic barking from the SPCA van. Then, out of the corner of his eye, he saw Emily climb onto a dumpster and swing herself onto the flat roof of the shed. Lying flat, she reached out her arms.

"Neil!" she yelled. With a huge effort that strained his wrists, Neil bundled the heavy dog into her arms, sure that Bully would be at his heels in a moment. But when he looked over his shoulder he saw Terri, Mike, and Gary hauling the raging dog away by his collar. Mike was struggling with a muzzle as Carl, in one last desperate effort, wrenched his way free from the officer holding him and dashed across the yard. The other police officers gave chase, but a shout from Sergeant Moorhead sent a lean gray shape tearing after him.

"It's Sherlock!" said Neil triumphantly, knowing Sherlock would do exactly the right thing. Sure enough, with a perfectly timed spring he seized Carl by the sleeve and held him, in spite of all the man's struggles, until Sergeant Moorhead and the other police officers were there to take over and march him to the police car. The car doors banged shut.

Neil looked around. It had all become strangely quiet. The dogfighting crowd, including Gary, had been taken away in various police cars. Terri and Mike were checking the dogs and pronouncing them unharmed.

"Physically, they're fine," said Mike. "I have no worries about Bramble, but he had a narrow escape. In time, he could have become thoroughly antisocial. As it is, he's scared, probably hungry, and on the defensive, but they haven't had time to wreck his temperament permanently. But as for Bully . . ." He looked at Terri, and shook his head.

Terri nodded. Then she turned to Neil and Emily. "I'll take you both home," she said. "Get ready for some major punishment from your parents."

"But on your way," said Sergeant Moorhead, "you could take the farm dog back to Priorsfield. There's no need to put him in a cell — he's put up with enough."

"The sooner he's home, the better," agreed Terri. All of a sudden, she looked desperately tired. She took out her cell phone and tapped in a number. In an instant, Neil heard his mother's voice as she answered.

"Carole?" said Terri. "Don't panic, everybody's all

right. I'm on my way to Priorsfield with Bramble and
Neil and Emily. Do you think you could come and
meet us there?"

Neil glanced at Emily and saw that they shared
the same thoughts. Sooner or later, they were going
to get an earful from one or both of their parents.

"We asked for it, I suppose," Emily sighed.

"It was worth it," said Neil.

"And we're going to Priorsfield," said Emily sensi-
bly. "They won't give us such a tongue-lashing in
front of the Greys. And by the time we get home,
they may have calmed down a bit."

Neil put an arm around Bramble, who didn't lick
him but didn't growl, either. "You've got me into trouble again," he said. "Never mind. You're still a great
dog."

CHAPTER TEN

By the time Neil and Emily reached Priorsfield Farm, it was completely dark. Harry and Angie Grey stood in the farmhouse doorway with the warm light of the hall behind them. Neil, jumping down from Terri's van, saw the King Street Kennels Range Rover arriving with his father at the wheel, and rushed over to try to get in his explanation first.

"Sorry, Dad," he said. "But —"

"I know," said Bob. "You were only trying to save a dog. You could have ruined a whole SPCA operation, not to mention putting yourself and Emily at risk. I'm glad to see you're each in one piece, but I'm still withholding your allowance and grounding you both for a week."

Neil and Emily exchanged worried looks.

"I suggest you get out of my sight before I think of something else," added Bob.

In Priorsfield Farm's kitchen, Harry Grey poured mugs of tea. Nick Christmas came over from his trailer.

"That solves the problem of who left Titan at Nick's trailer," said Terri. "Gary told us it was him. I've just spoken to Sergeant Moorhead, who said Gary was too scared to bring him to the vet, but he figured that somebody at the farm would take care of him. He usually believes everything Carl tells him, but he finally had his doubts about dogfighting."

"He usually *does* everything Carl tells him, let alone believes it," said Neil. "But he did care about Bramble. And Titan. Terri, did you find out anything about Titan? Like whether he has a real owner somewhere?"

"Titan, otherwise known as Rambo," said Terri. "I understand that Carl bought him in a diner two weeks ago from a man who kept him as a guard dog. The man decided that a guard dog was more trouble than it's worth. Burglar alarms don't have to be fed, exercised, and taken to the vet, so he sold the dog and bought a burglar alarm system instead. Carl thought he'd make a good fighter."

"Carl knows nothing about dogs," muttered Neil. "They're just a way of making money to him."

"Don't worry about Carl anymore, Neil," said

Terri. "He won't get near a dog where he's going, unless they use them to patrol the grounds. He's already on probation and he's got a criminal record. Sergeant Moorhead indicated to me that he'll definitely go to prison this time."

"And with Carl in jail, Gary might get his act together," said Bob.

"Gary must have some sense," admitted Neil. "He knew this was the right place for Bramble to be."

"It certainly is," said Harry Grey, and scratched Bramble's head. Bramble shook himself and went to the kitchen door, head to one side, whining softly.

"Oh, not more trouble." Emily sighed.

"No, I think he's just had enough of being indoors,"

said Harry. "Look at him — he's not a house dog. He wants his own kennel and his friend. Tuff will be glad to have him back. I'll take him out in a minute."

"What will happen to Bully?" asked Neil. He patted Jake, who was pawing at his knee for attention.

"Bully is what happens when you train a dog for fighting," said Terri sadly. "I'm sorry, Neil. It's my guess he's been trained for this kind of thing from when he was a puppy, and we can't change him now. The police might need to keep him for evidence, but then he'll almost certainly have to be put down."

Neil remembered Titan's scars, and nodded. "And what about Titan?" he said.

"Titan is going to be fine," said Terri, and allowed herself a smile. "He'll probably always be slow and he'll always limp, but he's behaved himself so far and he's been introduced to Sergeant Moorhead."

They'd almost forgotten Nick Christmas was there, but he spoke now. "Doesn't anybody want him, then?" he asked quietly. "I'll have him."

"Sorry, Nick," said Harry Grey in a tone of voice that would not allow argument. "No chance. Not while you're working here. I can't have him on a farm with sheep, especially at this time of year. He's trained to attack."

"Not much of a training," Neil pointed out. "They didn't have him long, and Mike says he's all right now."

"He's still a bull terrier with an aggressive streak," said Harry. "It's too risky, I'm afraid. It's out of the question. I'd be a fool to have him here. Have you ever seen the damage a dog can do among sheep?"

"Yes," said Neil, and nodded unhappily. It was a pity, though. Nick Christmas might have helped Titan calm down again. Soon it was time to go, but at the door, Neil turned. "Mr. Grey," he said, "would you like to meet Titan? Just to see how he's coming along?"

Harry Grey chuckled kindly. "Nice try, son, but it won't work. I'm not going to take one look at him and change my mind. Bring him if you want. I'd like to see how he's getting on, and if I can think of anyone who would take him, I'll let you know. But he's not staying here."

After school at the end of the following week, the Parkers returned to Priorsfield Farm. Sarah jumped out of the Range Rover, then Emily, and, finally, Neil. He turned and held out his arms for the dog that Carole carefully handed to him.

"You're staying on the leash now, Titan," he said as he gently put the dog down. "I know you're not fit enough to run anywhere, but this is a sheep farm, all the same."

Sarah, with a cry of "Where's my lamb?" ran to the fence and climbed up to look.

Harry Grey came out to meet them. "That one

there, playing King of the Castle on the rock. Can you see?" he said. "That's little Sarah."

"She's getting a lovely soft fleece," said Carole. "You won't need to knit her a blanket now, Sarah."

Sarah turned and gave her a grown-up look. "I'm not knitting blankets anymore," she said. "I've just finished my last one, and that's only a little one. It's my best one." From her pocket, she proudly took out a square of grubby and lopsided knitting the size of a matchbox.

"It's hamster-sized," she said. "It's for my pet hamster, Fudge." She returned it carefully to her pocket, and went to watch the lambs.

Neil and Emily walked back to the farmyard, adjusting to Titan's slow pace as he hobbled with determination beside them.

"Look," said Neil. "Have you seen the gate to the duck pond?"

"Oh, yes," said Emily. "There's a roll of chicken wire and a toolbox beside it. Harry must be adding some more wire to make it duck-proof!"

"And Tuff and Bramble!" cried Neil. "Together again!" The two dogs were chasing in and out of the hay bales as if Bramble had never been away. "It's great to see those two reunited!"

Tuff and Bramble, hearing their names, stopped their game and looked up. They growled a warning at Titan, who growled, too, but shrank back.

"Quiet, you two!" ordered Harry Grey as he joined them. "Let's take a better look at the invalid, then."

He bent to examine the pink scars on the dog's back and ran a gentle hand down the injured foreleg. Then he stood back, his chin in his hand. "He really is walking wounded, isn't he? I'm surprised Mike saved that leg at all. Give him a little walk up and down the yard for me, Neil."

That sounded hopeful, thought Neil as he walked slowly across the farmyard and back with Titan limping beside him. He glanced up now and then at Bramble and Tuff, who still growled, but didn't seem ready to attack. They had seen their master accept the strange dog.

"He'll get better than that," said Harry Grey, observing him, "but not much better. Oh, shut up, Tuff! Go and fetch the hammer if you want to show off! Tuff! Fetch the hammer!"

Neil remembered Tuff's old trick. Tuff ran straight to the toolbox, selected the hammer, and carried it back to Harry. It was an impressive piece of work, especially if you didn't know that whatever the farmer asked for, Tuff would always fetch the hammer. It was the only tool he liked.

As Tuff dropped the hammer at Harry's feet, a fluffy black duckling waddled inquisitively beneath the gate and stood in the farmyard, looking from side to side. Tuff sat watching it intensely with a

growl in his throat, but he now knew better than to go near it.

"Tuff's as brave as a lion with anything on four legs," said the farmer. "But he's not so sure about angry ducks that tumble out of the sky and peck him if he chases the little ones. It's not fair, is it, Tuff?"

Neil turned to see Nick Christmas ambling toward them, smiling. Carole and Sarah were behind him.

"Here's your dog, then, Nick," said Harry Grey. "Get him out from under my feet, will you?"

Bewildered, Nick looked from Harry to the dog to Neil. "But you said —" he began.

"I know what I said. But look at him, Nick, he

needs a walker. The sheep might see him coming and die laughing, but he won't harm them any other way."

"But . . ." repeated Nick as a smile spread across Neil's face.

"All the same, you're not to take any chances," the farmer went on. "Keep him on the leash or tethered, or in the trailer. If you want to let him have a good run — or a good limp, I should say — take him well away from the livestock."

"I will, boss, I will!" Nick's eyes were bright with joy as he stroked the dog's head. Titan sniffed at him and sat down at his feet. Neil smiled. Titan wasn't a dog for leaping, licking, and pawing, but by taking his place beside Nick, he'd made it clear that they'd get along. Neil watched them walk away together, the gruff old man and the tough white dog.

"Go on, then," Harry called after them, grinning. "Take him out of my way before I change my mind."

"Now we'll have to go," said Carole. "Sarah's got a ballet lesson and I think, Miss Sarah, you'd better go and change out of your dirty boots first."

"I'm nearly changed!" Sarah undid her coat and revealed a pink leotard underneath.

"Leotard and boots!" said Neil. "It'll never catch on. Can I just say goodbye to the dogs?"

He kneeled on the ground with Tuff and Bramble, admiring Bramble's spirit as he made little rushes at tumbling leaves.

"I wish none of this had happened," said Emily. "It's good that Bramble's home, and Nick and Titan have found each other, but I still wish it hadn't happened."

"Yes, I know." Neil held out the hammer and played tug-of-war with Tuff. "But we've been able to do something about it, so there'll be one less dog-fighting ring now." He stood up reluctantly as Carole, revving the engine, called them.

"Coming!" they both called.

Neil stole one last look over his shoulder. Bramble and Tuff were racing to the barn, and Titan and Nick Christmas, plodding toward the trailer, looked as if they had been together all their lives.